A Long Way From **Home**

by

Beverly Denise Thomas

When life comes *full circle*, you will realize
All you ever needed, *you already had*
You *just* refused to listen

iUniverse, Inc.
New York   Bloomington

A Long Way from Home
When Life Comes Full Circle, You Will Realize All You Ever Needed, You Already Had, You Just Refused to Listen

iUniverse books may be ordered through booksellers or by contacting:

iUniverse
1663 Liberty Drive
Bloomington, IN 47403
www.iuniverse.com
1-800-Authors (1-800-288-4677)

Because of the dynamic nature of the Internet, any Web addresses or links contained in this book may have changed since publication and may no longer be valid. The views expressed in this work are solely those of the author and do not necessarily reflect the views of the publisher, and the publisher hereby disclaims any responsibility for them.

ISBN: 978-1-4401-3367-1 (pbk)
ISBN: 978-1-4401-3368-8 (ebk)

Printed in the United States of America

iUniverse rev. date: 3/27/2009

This book is dedicated first and foremost to
my Lord and Saviour, Jesus Christ:

my parents, Lafayette and Louise Johnson
my children, Lafayette, Nichole,
Jasmine, Shawneice and Daniel
my companion, David
my church family, A Passion For Christ Ministries

1

FREEDOM

Almost Thanksgiving

Winter made her brisk arrival and gently settled in. Her fragrance was illuminated everywhere you gazed. All the trees were dressed in the finest of winter apparel, coupled with icicles and frost covering. The sun had been hidden from view for some few weeks, and many who embarked for work in the dark were embraced with the same darkness on the long journey back home to family and friends. It was almost Thanksgiving and time for family, friends, and trips to Granny's house.

Envisioned Freedom

Denise, like the prodigal son, was eager to vacate the family nest and begin her journey as an adult. She would be eighteen years old soon, and she had been planning her birthday for months. Denise had been contemplating and envisioning her "freedom." She thought of freedom as getting away from

Mom and Dad and being on her own. So many teens are seduced this way. Life is hard and often the "realness" of life is camouflaged by television, lies, and suggestions of friends. Parents' warnings often fade to the background once a teenager has his or her mind made up.

Denise believed that she knew *all* about life and was in control of her destiny. There would be no curfew, no rules to abide by, no more church, and no one to answer to.

Like Denise, the prodigal son **said to *his* father, Father, give me the portion of goods that falleth *to me*. And he divided unto them *his* living. And not many days after the young son gathered all together, and took his journey into a far country, and there wasted his substance with riotous [wasteful] living** (Luke 15:12-13).

Just Wait

"I can't wait until I am grown. I want to get out of this house and do my own thing. I won't have to listen to anyone. I want to be my own person." That's the shout going forth from many youth today. Many homes have been robbed of their teenage children due to such mentality. Not long ago, there was a newspaper article about the sister of a young man who had apparently committed suicide in his late teens. The young lady quietly commented, "I did not understand my parents when I was a teenager, but when I got older, around twenty years old, everything they said to me began to make sense. Just wait. Just wait. Just wait until you're twenty. It will all make sense then."

Have You Told Them?

It was her last year of high school, and Denise's primary focus was on leaving home. "Denise, did you tell your parents yet? Have you told them your plans?" asked Star, Denise's close friend.

"No," explained Denise. "They will find out when they find out. My dad might try and talk me out of it. You know how parents can be. My dad can't finish a complete thought without *talking about God. God. God. God.* But you know girl, when I get eighteen, ain't nothing or nobody tellin' me what to do. I'm gonna stay out until the sun comes up, date, and party *all* I want. *I will be free*. I feel like I am in prison now. I have to give an account of my every move. I can't even go alone to the corner store without getting the third degree. I am getting away from that place."

"I know," said DeShaun. "You've been talking to us about this every day. Day in and day out. 'I am getting out of that house.' That's all we've been hearing from you girl. I hope you got it all figured out because life ain't TV. You better give it plenty of thought."

"You guys are forgetting what I told you," whispered Carmen. "I left home, but now look at me. I could have finished high school, but no, I wanted to do my own thing. Now, it's taken me twice as long to get my high school diploma. I have to work while going to school. Do you know how hard that this? It seems to me that some things, no matter how much you are warned, will never sink in until you experience them. I'll tell you all to just wait and listen, but I know you won't listen, just like I didn't listen."

Everyone just looked at Carmen as if to say, "We ain't *you*, and that won't happen to us."

Sound Asleep

Denise had been discontented for what seemed like months. She even appeared to be depressed at times. There had been some fluctuations in her weight and sleeping habits. Her parents were concerned. While she was active in the church, she began to dread her time there. She could be found sound asleep during the tarrying services. While others were seeking the Holy Ghost baptism—*the old time power*—Denise was fast asleep.

Good or Bad

For where your treasure is, there will your heart be also (Luke 12:34). The heart is the vehicle that motivates you, good or bad. You can't conceal the intents of your heart. What's in you will *eventually* spill forth. **For out of the abundance of the heart the mouth speaketh** (Matthew 12:34).

Something Is Different

Denise's parents discussed her sudden change in attitude. "Something is different. Denise is changing. Her heart is somewhere else now. Her mannerisms are different. I believe she is seeing some young man," her mother Sheila stated with concern to William, her husband. "Sometimes she opens up and shares with me, but at other times, well, I just don't know what to make of it. She's becoming another person. I've tried to be a good mother to her, William. I've tried reaching out to her but she won't let me in."

"Oh, don't worry about it," William said. "You know how teenagers are. They are up and down. One day they love you, the next day, they believe they are ready to conquer Rome. She has all that she needs to make the right choices in life. It will now be up to her what she does with her life. It will be such a sad thing for her to travel the wrong road in life with so many opportunities before her."

"Last week upon arriving at the church, I asked her what had taken her so long," Sheila commented. "I knew she was not being truthful with me. She stated that she had walked and that was what had taken her so long. William, Denise has never wanted to walk anywhere. We are talking about 'Princess Denise.'"

If You Put Out Bad

Time has a way of *unwrapping* the truth. Mysteries once locked in decades of time have been solved. Children must be taught to do what's right by God and others. The Bible has always been clear about this.

Be not deceived; God is not mocked: for *whatsoever* a man soweth, that shall he also reap (Galatians 6:7). God has promised that if you put out good, good will come back to you, and if you put out bad, that's just what you will reap.

For he that soweth to his flesh shall of the flesh reap corruption; but he that soweth to the Spirit shall of the Spirit reap life everlasting (Galatians 6:8).

Malcolm's Surprise

Denise, so intoxicated with the idea of being on her own, had been sneaking around seeing Malcolm Whalen, a young man who was ten years her senior.

Malcolm's day consisted of getting up, hanging on the local street corner, smoking drugs and lying with any young lady that would give him the time of day. In other words, he was *trouble*.

Malcolm had a surprise waiting for Denise. She went out of her way to get him to notice her. "Malcolm," shouted Denise, as she exited a local cab. "What's up? I've been looking for you," she continued.

"Yeah, you've been lookin' for me for what? I don't take up with *jail bait*," he stated.

"I ain't no jail bait, and as a matter of fact, I'm going to be a *real* woman in just a few days. Now, what you got to say about that?" smirked Denise.

"When you get legal, come back, and we'll hook up … and … *you know*," laughed Malcolm. "Hey, I gotta go. Got stuff to do, places to go. Come back when you be a woman."

"Oh, I'll be back. I'll be back all right, and I'll be free to do what I want to do. You'll see," thought Denise. They parted, and headed in separate ways, and all the while Denise's mind was overwhelmed with ideas—ideas of freedom and ideas of being a woman. "Just a few more days and I'll be free, free to make my own choices in life. After all, I'm young and pretty," thought Denise. "I am going to leave my mark on this world. I'll show them. I'll show them all that I can take care of myself." She was late, late … once again. She rushed home.

Denise's Last Thanksgiving

Denise spent her last Thanksgiving with her family. "Happy Thanksgiving! Happy Thanksgiving!" everyone shouted to one another as they embraced for Thanksgiving dinner. Sharon, Juanita, Tyrone, Mattie, and some other friends of Denise were in attendance at this last Thanksgiving dinner.

Sharon whispered, "Hey Denise, just a few more days and you will be free. How you gonna do it, you know? How are you tellin' your parents? That's going to be something. I just wish that I could be a *fly on the wall*."

"Oh, be quiet Sharon. Stop encouraging her to do wrong. You're still at home with your parents. None of us, and I do mean not one of us, knows what it is like to be on our own. Our friends, you know, they are always telling lies about what they have. How do you know that what Denise has heard from others, even from Malcolm, is not just a pack of lies?" argued DeShaun. Denise and Sharon stood dazed and offered DeShaun nothing, nothing but frowns.

Life Is Hard

DeShaun continued, "Nothing is what it seems. Life is hard. If that wasn't the case, there wouldn't be so much trouble in the world. There wouldn't be so many homeless people, so many people unemployed—so many broken homes—so many sick folk. Open your eyes and stop living in Wonderland."

"That's enough. Both of you be quiet," Denise said. "I've made my decision, and I am going through with it. I have it all planned out. I made arrangements for my cousin "Z" to come with her husband to get my stuff. Little by little, I have been cleaning out my closet and throwing stuff away. When I get out of this house, I am going to *get busy.* I am going to get me a man, get me a job, and get my own place. Oh, I can't wait. They will be shocked at what I'm gonna do. I can just imagine their faces, especially my dad, but so what?"

Dear Lord

"Okay, okay, who's going to say grace?" Sheila asked, as they all sat down to dinner. "Denise, why don't you do it?"

"Sure. Dear Lord, thank you for this wonderful dinner, but most of all I thank you for *people that really love me*. I thank you for all of my family and friends. Thank you for this wonderful meal, a meal that I am sure *we will never, never forget*. Amen."

Everyone said, "Amen."

The turkey, dressing, ham, and greens were passed around to the fully seated table. Not one empty seat was visible. Each face was glazed over with excitement. There was Christmas music covering all the walls and much anticipation filled the room about what would be placed on the table next. While plates were packed with favorites, family members looked ahead. "Can't wait for dessert," commented Nicole.

"*Bam that ham*, William Whiting," laughed Denise's classmate, Star. "I am always ready for William's ham. Bring it on. Bring it on."

Eating Themselves to Sleep

The evening progressed with joy and an abundance of excitement obviously flowed from Denise. "The game is on. The game is on," many of the men exclaimed. "What room? What room? Let's watch it on the big TV downstairs in William's recreational room," commented one of the guests. All the guys then proceeded downstairs for an evening of sports activity while others continued to play board games or simply eat themselves into oblivion.

As the evening continued, family members, Sharon and Juanita said their goodbyes. "Goodnight everyone. We are going to roll ourselves home now," commented Juanita.

"Everything was so wonderful, Sheila," stated Sharon. They headed home. Soon the house was near empty. The games were over and everyone was pushing for home and to bed.

"Goodnight all, and thanks for coming," said William and Sheila. "Be careful going home and watch out," concluded William.

What's Up?

William and Sheila completed the cleaning of the house, along with the children, Denise, Victoria, and Marcus. They all unwound, and sighs could be heard ringing forth from the various bedrooms. There was a slow, gradual walk toward William and Sheila's bedroom. "Who is that?" asked Sheila. "Who's still walking around out there?" William asked sluggishly.

"It's me," commented Denise.

"Me who?" shouted Sheila. "Oh, it's you, Denise. I thought you were fast asleep by now. You look stuffed. What's up?"

Denise attempted to say something but instead muttered, "You know, it's late and I wanted to talk to you and Dad about something, but it can wait until tomorrow." Both William and Sheila watched the doorway as Denise strolled back to her room. They pondered what it might have been that Denise wanted to talk to them about. Too tired to give it another thought, William and Sheila shrugged their shoulders, turned off the lights and fell fast asleep.

No Man Gave unto Him

What was so important to Denise? In just a few days, she would be eighteen. Did it have something to do with turning eighteen? What was it? Would she, like the prodigal son, insist on claiming her right to leave home? Remember the prodigal son? He continued his journey. **And when he had spent all, there arose a mighty famine in that land; and he began to be in want. And he went and joined himself to a citizen of that country; and he sent him into his fields to feed swine. And he would fain have filled his belly with the husks that the swine did eat: and no man gave unto him** (Luke 15:14-16).

Enter ye in at the strait gate: for wide is the gate, and broad *is* the way, that leadeth to destruction, and many there be which go in thereat: Because strait *is* the gate, and narrow *is* the way, which leadeth unto life, and few there be that find it (Matthew 7:13-14).

The Real World

Life is full of surprises. You can often become blinded by your own desires. Crowded by the false opinions of others, the blurred view of television and the fabricated tales of others, you can become unaware and unprepared for the real world. God provides good parents to train, lead, and guide you so that you won't make the same mistakes that your parents made. Any good parent wants his or her children to do better, to be better, and to go farther in life than he or she did.

The Bible, our guide and road map, is stuffed with examples for us to follow. There are examples and illustrations of those who stayed with God and were rewarded, and there are the escapades of those who lived foolish lives, wasting their money and never mounting up to be what God intended for them to be. Mercifully, some have tasted the so called "*good life*" and survived to tell others, "It's not what you think. Stay with God. Stay home. Keep your virginity until your wedding night. Stay in school. Get your education. Do something with your life. There will be time. There will be time for all that other stuff."

Life Is Hard

Life is hard, and you are guaranteed problems. We live in very troubling times. Even in the midst of all that is going on, you still have the precious commodity of *free choice*. That is what you will be judged by, and that is what you will have to answer for. Remember, you will have to live with the every decision that you make in your life.

2

THE DEPARTURE

You're Eighteen!

"Happy birthday to you. Happy birthday to you. Happy birthday, dear Denise. Happy birthday to you."

"Thanks mom and dad. There's nothing like being awakened by the sound of your parents' singing," stated Denise.

"Well today you are eighteen years old and no longer *momma's little girl*," explained Sheila.

"Well, you know you will always be our little girl," commented William.

Hi Dad, It's Me

William and Sheila left the house to run errands and take care of business. This was often their Saturday routine. It was mid-afternoon when William's cell phone rang. "Hello," answered William.

"Hi Dad, it's me."

"Hey Denise, I mean 'birthday girl,' what's up?" asked William.

"Well," hesitated Denise. "I wanted. Well, what I am trying to say is, I wanted to tell you this in person. Dad, I have tried to tell you, but you wouldn't … well, I could never talk to you."

"Denise, what is this all about? What are you trying to say?" questioned William.

I Am Moving Out Today

"I am moving out today," Denise stated.

"What are you talking about Denise? You're moving out, where?" shouted William.

"William, what is it? What is Denise talking about? What is the problem?" Sheila asked.

"Just one minute, Sheila," commented William. "Now, Denise, what are you talking about; you tried to talk to me?"

Denise handed the telephone to "Z." "William, hi, it's Z. Denise told me she tried to talk to you on more than one occasion, but you simply would not listen. Now William, this is your daughter, and I don't understand what went wrong between you two, but my husband and I are on our way to the house to get Denise and her belongings. I understand that she is packed up and ready to go," concluded Z.

"Let me talk to my daughter Z! Let me talk to Denise. Put Denise back on the telephone!"

Don't Leave Home

There was a moment of silence as William attempted to regain his composure. The intensity of it all caused William to breathe funny—he couldn't catch his breath—and his eyes were enveloped with tears. "Denise, wait. Denise, please wait for me to get home. Let's talk this over. We can work this out. Don't leave home. Don't leave home, not like this. Please, not like this." William hung up the telephone.

Sheila watched with great fear as William navigated home. While he was driving, it was obvious his mind was *caught up* with other thoughts. *How could this have happened? How did I miss this? What have I done? Why is she leaving me?* These were the questions that surrounded William's mind. On and on went the guilt. It seemed to grow like an out-of-control balloon, just waiting to explode with the slightest touch.

All Things Made Ready

"Let's go home. I have to get home, Sheila."

Sheila was stunned and didn't know what to say to William. Very few words passed between them during the tedious ride home. The car was barely parked when William emerged from the vehicle and raced upstairs in an attempt to speak with Denise. Certainly, many thoughts flooded his mind. Sheila felt helpless and uneasy as she watched William's final attempt to reach Denise, but it could be felt from the moment that William and Sheila entered the house—*all things had been made ready*. Denise had no intention of changing her mind. She was determined. William and Sheila would discover in the weeks to come that Denise had been planning and calculating her "*escape*" for months.

Shut the Door

Three weeks prior to Denise's leaving home, Sharon paid her a visit. "Hi, Sheila, is Denise home?"

"Yes, go right in the back. You know where her room is," commented Sheila as Sharon proceeded down the long hallway, which led to Denise's room.

Sharon knocked on the closed door. "Hey Denise, let me in."

"Oh, hey, hurry up and shut the door before somebody comes back here," said Denise. "I am throwing out all this stuff. I won't need any of this junk anyway. These clothes always made me look like a little girl. Those days are over."

"Give me another garbage bag so that I can help you," commented Sharon. "Hey I like this. Can I have it?"

"No. Throw it all away."

"Well, one thing is for sure, your room has never been this clean," chuckled Sharon.

"Oh, don't be so smart. Help me so that we can get done."

No Set Rules

As parents, there are no set rules. Parents can only teach their children what they have learned. *It then becomes the responsibility of the young adult to do better when they are able.* It is much more difficult when there are stepchildren and stepparents involved. The stepparents attempt to perform an *almost* insurmountable task—assume the role of the missing parent. What brought about the new family structure? Was it divorce? Was it death? What led to the new union? How were the children affected? Does a viable relationship still exist with both biological parents? The stepparent is often left to shoulder these burdens, particularly if the child is of significant age when the new family structure is formed.

Parents need God to help them right from the very beginning. In many cases, the parents come from stepfamilies or dysfunctional homes. We must hold one another high and pray much for the family structure in this last and final hour. After all, we are our godly brother's keeper. The enemy has set his mind against the survival of the family. There is a barrage of influences working against the success of the family structure. Unsupervised watching of television is one. Many parents see this as "time out" for the child. Others use computers. Both of these *can be fatal*. There are some programs, even cartoons, where the characters talk back and disrespect their parents. Some of the videos games out now are infiltrated with great degrees of violence, sex, and drugs. We have to be ever so careful. Recently, a newscast noted that many of our young teenage girls become pregnant as a result of the increased promiscuity rate on television. They want what they see portrayed on television. Television, in so many cases, presents falsehoods—not the real thing. It is *full* of fantasy and make-believe.

Denise Wanted Her Father

Denise came to live with her father, William and his wife, Sheila, when she had already begun to embark on those teenage years. She had already experienced so much. There were scars to heal and wounds, which needed mending.

William and Sheila had other children upon Denise's arrival in their home, and there were many adjustments required. Denise wanted *her* father. She needed her father, but so did Sheila and her children. William was a breath of fresh air to Sheila and her children. Sheila's children reached out and gravitated toward William. He was what they had longed for—what had been missing from their lives. There was much change to be embraced by all. Change can be difficult.

It Doesn't Matter About the Past

The mistakes are of no importance. Who, in this life, has not made mistakes? No, it doesn't matter about the past. What matters is love. When you have love, love will win over each and every situation. **For charity [love] shall cover the multitude of sins [faults]** (I Peter 4:8a).

God seeks to heal families, but families must be *willing* to *give love a chance*. William, Sheila, and even Denise were not consistent in communicating. It was on again, off again. Denise felt betrayed by the fact that her father had to be shared. Sheila felt stuck in the middle, unable to really give godly discipline to Denise because of possible rejection from William. It was *almost impossible*, but again love was not given its proper chance. Where was the balance?

Why Waste Time?

The mother and father who care for you right now may not be the man and woman God used to bring you into this world. Take advantage of what is before you. Why waste a lifetime blaming others for your problems? Guess what? This life is full of troubles and obstacles. Be ready to face life head on. We live in very troubling times. We all have problems. Since the fall of Adam, we have *all* been misused, mistreated, abandoned, or rejected. It was only when Christ became the bridge back to God that a way was made for every man, woman, boy, and girl to reunite in harmony. People who try to exist outside of this "Eden"—this Eden given to us through the shed blood of Jesus Christ—are missing the mark. They are simply off course.

Do you, like Denise, harbor something in your heart against your parents? What good will it do for you in the end? Have you been the perfect child, mother, or father? Well then, lets give love a chance. What do you think about that? Everybody *needs* love. Why, look at you—living like a pauper, when you could be rich, rich with God's love. You're missing out on so much.

The Driving Force

Except the Lord build the house, they labour in vain that build it: except the Lord keep the city, the watchman waketh *but* in vain (Psalm 127:1).

Jesus Christ must be the driving force used to raise our children. His precious blood was given as a bridge back to love, back to harmony. Much was lost in the fall of Adam. That wonderful harmony that existed in the Garden of Eden was destroyed when Adam disobeyed God. It would take the second Adam, Jesus Christ, to build a highway for all families to exist. There is no family without love. ***There is no love without Christ.***

Longing and Yearning

For he satisfieth the longing soul, and filleth the hungry soul with goodness (Psalm 107:9). Since the fall of Adam, each person on planet Earth has been longing and yearning for his or her maker. We each carry a part of God within. **And the Lord God formed man *of* the dust of the ground, and breathed into his nostrils the breath of life; and man became a living soul** (Genesis 2:7).

False Love

The soul came from God, and it longs for its maker. Many don't recognize this longing as coming from God, and therefore, they respond to some false love—some counterfeit, which often leads to destructive behavior.

Since God made us and gave us a part of Him—the ***soul***—we long for the one who made us. We long for God, for God is love. *We are creatures who cannot exist without love.* We can go days without water and even weeks without food, but we will not thrive properly without love. We will do bad things and say bad things when that love is absent from our lives—absent from our hearts.

Are you, like Denise, longing for love? What drives your ambitions and goals? Do you find satisfaction in dressing provocatively? Do you love and long for money, material gain, and attention? Why child, you are simply *yearning* for love, God's love. Why not be made whole? Will thou be made whole?

For we know that the whole creation groaneth and travaileth in pain together until now (Romans 8:22).

Look how much time you've wasted. It's time to turn to love!

Are You Taking Your Book Bag?

Sharon and Denise finished packing. "Denise, you are throwing away a lot of stuff. Did you tell Z what day to come for you?" asked Sharon.

"Yes, she has all the information. I am just waiting for that day," commented Denise.

"Hey, what's this? It is your book bag. Are you taking this with you? What's in there anyway? It's very heavy."

"Don't open it. *It's not important.* Where I am going, I won't need it. Just leave it here. They can do whatever they want with it. I don't care. I am glad to be rid of it and its contents," concluded Denise. They finished packing and left the house for some lunch.

Satisfaction in Suffering

William finally made it home and frantically entered the door and rushed into Denise's room. She was all packed and sitting on her bed. Her face was filled with sternness and an uncompromising expression. It would seem that she had rehearsed this moment—that she had predicted William's response, anticipated and even longed for the hurt, which flushed in his frightful face. With each word that William poured forth in anguish and desperation, Denise felt gratified, justified. She felt satisfaction in his suffering. She was delighted as Denise looked still-faced into William's tear-filled eyes. She seemed to be without feelings. Denise poured forth with a mocking, bitter spirit. It was too hard to watch. Her eyes were all aglow, not with joy but with revenge, anger, and hostility. She displayed this arrogance as William emptied himself at her feet.

Time's Cruel Joke

Time had played a cruel joke on William and didn't allow him an opportunity to gain his composure before the doorbell rang. Like Job, William's day of reckoning had made its arrival. It was Z and her husband, and of course, Sheila had to open the door. The house was immersed in all kinds of uncertain emotions. Sheila was angry and confused, all at the same time. She buzzed Z and her husband into the building and listened as they mounted the stairs to the third floor apartment. William raced toward Sheila and wondered why she had let them in.

"William, we can't act like this. It is obvious that Denise has been planning this for a long time. William, just let her go. Please, just let her go."

"You didn't have to let them in, Sheila."

"William, please let her go. What was I suppose to do? Act in such a way as to validate all that they have been told about us? No, William, let her go. Please let her go," pleaded Sheila.

Eyes Full of Tears

Z and her husband entered the home. With eyes full of tears, William attempted to compose himself as he took Denise's belongings down to the waiting car. He was certainly a dead man walking that day. Only God knows how William was able to move about. Z's husband was stellar, tall, and handsome. They complemented each other well. It was obvious from their demeanor that they expected some confrontation, but there was none from William or Sheila. Denise said her goodbyes to Sheila. Sheila was sitting down, facing toward her computer. She halfway turned to say goodbye, and then Denise *was gone*. Yes, Denise was gone but *gone* from what to what? Would life play out like she thought? Would she live out her dreams? At that moment, Denise had all the answers *or so she thought*.

Finally, Denise was all packed up and in the Z's car. Sheila watched with heartfelt sympathy for William. She was lost at how to help him. William waved as the car spun off. *She was gone* her way to live her life. It would be several weeks before William could bring himself to speak to Denise. She wanted what she wanted, and William needed time. He needed time—just time.

Questions

Questions flooded the atmosphere for the remainder of the evening. William was so unsettled, moving about from room to room. Finally, William sat down, and Sheila grabbed him and held him as he cried. William attempted to sleep, but sleep refused him comfort. "If I could just fall asleep. By morning I will wake up and see that this is just a bad dream," William attempted to reason within himself. No, William would soon discover just how real this episode of his life was.

After sometime, he went about the house. It was obvious he was confused. He found himself in Denise's room. For a moment, he just stood in the middle of the floor. Memories of the first day she came to live with William flooded his mind. Her eighth-grade graduation, birthdays, outings—all came crashing down on him. William fell to the floor and sobbed. Finally, he came to himself and slothfully emerged from the floor. Like a drunken man, William climbed from the floor. The sighs could be heard all over the silent house.

How Could She?

William looked through the dresser drawers and opened the closet door. Some clothes were still hanging on the hangers. A dress from a previous graduation, books from school, and tokens given to Denise were all left behind as if to make a statement. William was just too distraught to attempt to interpret what that statement might be.

On the floor of the closet was Denise's book bag. She had left it behind. How could she? She felt no need for its contents. Had she mastered all lessons encased within her book bag? Did Denise become a master of life? No, Denise had no clue of how valuable the contents of the book bag were. Somewhere down the road, she would long for the *contents* of her book bag. She would hunt for them, and regret leaving them behind.

For now, though, she was ignorant of her great, great need of its contents. William grabbed and held onto the book bag. He held it close as if he were embracing a small child after the return home from a long trip. William once again began to sob. Sheila stayed in the other room and left William to deal with his feelings of what had just happened.

Somber Days Ahead

There were many somber days ahead. William and Sheila spent much time reflecting on what could have led to Denise's desire to leave home. Had all been done to show love toward Denise? Did William and Sheila work hard at keeping the lines of communication open? These and more questions surfaced from both Sheila and William. Sheila, as she reflected on her actions, concluded that she could have done more to reach Denise.

Even though it was awkward at times, Sheila admitted that she could have done more. William always felt that Denise was troubled by the fact that he had not been there for her in earlier years. You see, Denise didn't come to know her father until she was ten or eleven years old, and by that time, William had a *ready-made* family. Where would the time come from for Denise? She wanted her father to herself. She wanted all of his attention, but now that was impossible. Denise's reasons for leaving the home may never be uncovered, but William and Sheila felt it necessary to take self-evaluations and make changes to avoid this from ever happening to any of the other children, if possible. This self-evaluation, of course, was no guarantee. So many young adults are lured into the so-called "good life" at no fault of their parents.

Unwarranted Guilt

During the months to follow, William learned the extent of Denise's discontentment. Others, whom Denise had confided in, saw the misery and anguish which haunted William and, in an effort to relieve him of some unwarranted guilt, began to tell him of Denise's plans. Many shared with William about Denise's desire for another life, a life different from that displayed by William and Sheila. This news brought William and Sheila some minimal solace. Denise left home, according to the others, because she wanted a life that was different than the one she was offered. The life she had chosen—the life she had been told about by her friends and circle of acquaintances—was enticing and captivating. Denise felt like she was missing life. Sometimes a son or a daughter will talk about their mother and father and say *they don't want to be like them*, even though they may have their characteristics. So many will despise a personality so much like their own. This is dangerous.

At William and Sheila's house, living for God was paramount. Attending the services was very important. How you conducted yourself was important. It was emphasized to all the children that, no matter what others were doing, following God was the standard. Every person was free, at the age of eighteen, to move on if they felt the need to live differently. While serving God was not forced on anyone, all would be respectful, attend services, perform chores, and adhere to curfew.

William was strong in the faith and strongly encouraged his children to find themselves in Christ. He gave examples from the Bible about those who were successful because of giving their lives to Christ. William also, through the scriptures, reminded his children of the youth in the Bible, such as Timothy and Jeremiah. They remained faithful to God. There were others that William would allude to in speaking with the children.

Then there was Achan. He was completely destroyed because of *what he wanted.* He wanted to have what God said, "Thou shalt not!" It cost Achan everything. He *lost everything* and was never able to enjoy the spoils of disobedience.

The fancy clothes, worldly songs, and lifestyles of others were prohibited in the home. Living for God was not *forced* upon anyone, but both Sheila and William were examples for their children.

Sheila Instructed the Children

There wasn't a lot of money, and the money that was there would not be squandered away. Sheila instructed the children in the Sunday school lessons each week, and the children fasted, along with their parents. There was careful scrutiny over where they went and who they talked to on the telephone and on outgoing engagements. While William and Sheila did not deter them from all school and social activities, the children were allowed to participate in only a selected few. Those school programs, which advocated rap, dancing, or the like, were not approved. The children were not allowed to "just do anything," but structured engagements were preferred. There was no television on school days. Again, there were chores and responsibilities allocated to each child.

Merely Existing

For several months, William and Sheila merely existed. William often thought of Denise and wondered how things had turned out for her, but he refused to contact her. He wanted Denise to experience freedom. This was what she had planned for. She had longed for freedom, and William wanted her to be free without his interference. Denise had planned with precision her day of freedom, and it had come.

William didn't want Denise to feel like he was hounding her or trying to get her to return home. There was a very stringent policy at William and Sheila's house. You could stay as long as you wanted, just as long as you did something with yourself. You either went to school or you worked. However, if you left home wrong, you could never return there and live.

It's Just a Bad Dream

"Oh, God please help me! Oh, oh God please help me! Help! Help! Where is Denise? Don't let anything happen to my baby. Oh, God please!"

"William!" shouted Sheila. "William!" She was shaking his shivering, wet body in an attempt to wake him from this deep madness. William's face was covered with tears. He was gripping his soaked and enshrouded pillow with all his might. "William, wake up! William, it's me, Sheila. Sweetie, please wake up. You're having a bad dream." Sheila grabbed William and held him. "William, hold on. Hold on."

"Denise. Where is Denise? She doesn't know what's ahead. She doesn't know about the world, the mean, mean world. She is so pretty and naïve. Someone may use her and even hurt her. I couldn't bear that. People are not what they appear to be," cried William.

"It's just a bad dream. It's just a bad, bad dream," whispered Sheila, as she rocked *her* William.

3

ABDUCTED!

There is a way that seemeth right unto a man; but the end thereof are the ways of death (Proverbs 16:25).

What Is This Place?

"Where am I? I am cold. What? Why are my hands tied behind my back? Oh, I can't move. There's blood. My body is sore. I feel like a truck hit me. Oh, my God, my mouth has been taped shut! What is this place? It's dark, and I don't know this place. How did I even get here? I was out on a date with Malcolm. He's not responsible for this, is he? I wonder if they took him, too. My God, what if he's dead?" My parents—my dad—he doesn't know where I am.

Held Captive

Denise suddenly heard footsteps, which seemed to be approaching the dark, frigid door, which held her captive. The room was covered in darkness, and it was hard to determine where she was. Was she in someone's basement or was this an abandoned house? She couldn't tell.

With each movement, she experienced severe pain in the lower part of her body, in between her thighs; something had been done to her. Maybe she had been in an accident. She was wailing from the residue of what seemed to be some drug stimulant. She was confused and disoriented. Had she been drugged? But she had just been with Malcolm. Her main reason for leaving home was to be with Malcolm. *She wanted him to be her first.* She disobeyed her parents for him. Denise lied so she could be with him. She had left God … yes, left God for Malcolm. He wasn't there when she needed him. If he, too, were dead…. Now, Denise was out the home she had grown up in. She was all alone. This was not what Denise had planned for. What now?

I Don't Deal with Jailbait!

"Hello, this is Malcolm, who is this?"

"This is Denise. You don't recognize my voice?"

"Oh, are you legal now? You know I don't deal with jailbait."

"Well, why do you think I'm calling? I'm on my own now and wanted to get together with you."

"You sure you know what you doin,' girl? I ain't got time to play no games with kids. You ready for this?"

"Yeah, I'm ready. I've been ready."

Remember, Denise had gone out of her way to get Malcolm to notice her. She promised him she would be back when she was legal. Well, now she was legal.

It had been nearly seven months since Denise said she would "make her mark on the world."

Experience Freedom

William and Sheila had begun to experience some sense of normalcy in their lives. So many questions were still left unanswered, but they had determined to let Denise make her own decisions, her own choices in life. William chose not to contact Denise but to give her the time she had longed for. He wanted her to experience the freedom she deserted home for. William was neither angry with Denise nor resentful. He simply could not understand *the way* she left. He would not have stopped her from leaving when she turned eighteen. *But the way it was done.* Well, it was a done deal now.

Reflecting on Denise's departure, both William and Sheila committed to more family time. Children have to be diligent about getting their parents to *hear* them, and parents must be diligent about *listening* to their children. If you don't listen to your children, they will find someone who will, but what will they be told? Topics such as dating, marriage, intercourse, drugs, and the like should be taught in home and not in some alley. So many homes are ill-equipped to help their children in these matters. The church has to step up and *stand in the gap*.

In the Dark

As Denise sat in the still, thick darkness, she began to reflect on the events of the last few days with Malcolm. It seemed so wonderful. She had begun to rejoice about all the decisions she had made. She finally began to *feel* free. Day after day, she and Malcolm spent a lot of time together. They would go places that Denise's parents never allowed her to go. Denise was her own person and did just what she wanted to do. The *tension* and *struggle* within was over. *She had won*. She knew it!

Hellfire and Brimstone

All she had to do was get out of that house. She would sit in the services and feel strong conviction as those *hellfire and brimstone* messages flashed before her eyes. It seemed as if the preacher had been following her around, like a detective, monitoring her every move.

At times, she thought she would break free from the clutches of the enemy and run, run for the altar, but that feeling only lasted momentarily. Soon Denise would *come to herself* and realize it must be a trick to get young people to leave the world and *grow old before their time*, but she was *up on that*. She couldn't be fooled. She wouldn't be fooled.

Once, to keep those influences from getting in her mind, she pretended to be praying, but actually she was asleep. While the praises were going before the throne of God, as sincere hearts sought the *old time* power, Denise was asleep. Her heart had become hardened to the word of God. When a heart becomes hardened, a person will commit sin and then go to church, convincing people that they are all right with God. Serving God had become a chore. Denise would use it as a weapon to get favors from her parents. Denise figured if they thought she was seeking God, she could get whatever she wanted. Oftentimes, she was granted favors from both William and Sheila. They would do anything to help encourage Denise to serve God. They, however, were not "buying" her love. Either she loved them or she didn't. *Real* love can't be counterfeited.

For we wrestle not against flesh and blood, but against principalities, against powers, against the rulers of the darkness of this world, against spiritual wickedness in high *places* (Ephesians 6:12).

The Battle Raging Within

Denise felt such a battle raging within. Two forces fought to possess her. She summed it up as the need to leave home and be on her own. Denise would mix and mingle with that which was ungodly and then go home and pray with the family. She had been sneaking off and indulging in the wrong things. While she hadn't lost her virginity, she was playing with sin, seeing how close she could get without going all the way. It was such a battle within as she tried to do both, but it would never work. She had to choose, and she chose the world.

No man can serve two masters: for either he will hate the one, and love the other; or else he will hold to the one, and despise the other. Ye cannot serve God and mammon (Matthew 6:24).

She had to break free. Once Denise left home, it seemed as if her mind became clearer. The struggle had ended.

Dearly beloved, I beseech you as strangers and pilgrims, abstain from fleshly lusts, which war against the soul (I Peter 2:11).

From whence *come* wars and fightings among you? C*ome they* not hence, *even* of your lusts that war in your members? Ye lust, and have not: ye kill, and desire to have, and cannot obtain: ye fight and war, yet ye have not, because ye ask not. Ye ask, and receive not, because ye ask amiss, that ye may consume *it* upon your lusts (James 4:1-3).

King David

Like King David, Denise thought she was free. David had a man killed to get what he wanted. His mind became more and more tormented with each devilish step he took. There would be no satisfaction until David had orchestrated a man's murder. He went after something when God said, "Thou Shalt Not!"

And it came to pass, after the year was expired, at the time when kings go forth *to battle*, that David sent Joab, and his servants with him, and all Israel; and they destroyed the children of Ammon, and besieged Rabbah. But David tarried still at Jerusalem (2 Samuel 11:1).

And it came to pass in an eveningtide, that David arose from off his bed, and walked upon the roof of the king's house: and from the roof he saw a woman washing herself; and the woman *was* very beautiful to look upon. And David sent and enquired after the woman. And *one* said, *Is* not this Bathsheba, the daughter of Eliam, the wife of Uriah the Hittite? (2 Samuel 11:2–3).

You Are the Man

And the LORD sent Nathan unto David. And he came unto him, and said unto him, There were two men in one city; the one rich, and the other poor. The rich *man* had exceeding many flocks and herds (2 Samuel 12:1–2).

And David's anger was greatly kindled against the man; and he said to Nathan, *As* the LORD liveth, the man that hath done this *thing* shall surely die: And he shall restore the lamb fourfold, because he did this thing, and because he had no pity. And Nathan said to David, Thou *art* the man (2 Samuel 12:5-7).

The Lord had granted David much in his lifetime, but David wanted to take that which God said, "Thou Shalt Not." When a mind is not subjected to the will of God, it will long and crave for the things of this old world, things that will ultimately destroy that person. David didn't know who he was. If he had, he would have recognized himself when Nathan approached him. The great secret of serving God and doing His whole will, to know what separation is, what dedication is, what justification is, what consecration is, and to know how to fit the Word to yourself is to know yourself. Are you a stranger to yourself? Do you know others better than you know yourself? David—King David didn't know who he was. Unless you know yourself, you'll think you're pleasing God when you're not. In order to keep from being afraid, you must know yourself and face it if you have fear.

God Cannot Be Tempted

Let no man say when he is tempted, I am tempted of God: for God cannot be tempted with evil, neither tempteth he any man: But every man is tempted, when he is drawn away of his own lust, and enticed. Then when lust hath conceived, it bringeth forth sin: and sin, when it is finished, bringeth forth death. Do not err, my beloved brethren (James 1:13-16).

When Sin Is Done with You

The enemy used the same tactics on Denise that he used on King David—lust and temptation. Lust of the eyes, temptation, and ego were his weapons.

Many are drawn into the **wrong** things by the **wrong** desires and **wrong** beliefs. The devil will entice young people to engage in unholy dating—handling each other's bodies and pretending that if you go all the way you will still be all right with God. *You won't be completely satisfied until you go all the way*, and then what? *When sin is done with you, then what?* Sex is like that.

History tells us that David "bleached his bones in prayer." Down through the years, he was considered "a man after God's own heart." The Bible does not tell us if David got the heart of God, only that he sought God for it. The Lord restored David *but he paid a great, great* price. His entire family suffered for **his** actions.

Denise would have to learn this lesson **the hard way**. Would she even survive life's cruel, cruel teachings?

Meet Me Outside

"Hey, Denise, meet me outside in fifteen minutes. I want to take you somewhere."

"Malcolm, where are you taking me? Oh, it doesn't matter—you've been such a gentleman so far." Denise rushed to get dressed and met Malcolm as planned.

Malcolm pulled up in a dark blue and grey conversion van, not his car. Denise never gave it another thought. "Got a new car?"

"No, just borrowed it for tonight."

"What do we need a van for?"

"You'll see. You'll see, baby girl," commented Malcolm.

Malcolm's cell phone rang. "Hey, what's up?" he said.

The voice on the other end said, "You got the goods?"

"Yeah, I got it."

"Everything's still on?"

"Yeah, you know me, Dog."

"Just have everything all set."

"See you at the place, Dog."

"I'll be there and I'll be waiting."

Malcolm rushed to say, "Hey, hey, remember to tell *the man* that this is it. Don't forget to tell him, Dog."

The person on the other end said, "Yeah, yeah, take that up with him, on your time, but as for me, bring me my stuff!"

Malcolm was a drug dealer who now wanted out. Did he think it would be so easy? Do you think that you can play around with the devil and just get out of the game without paying? Think again.

You Sought Me Out

Denise calmly said, "What's that all about?"

Malcolm figured he would tell Denise more about himself. She really didn't know him. Denise had only known of Malcolm what she had imagined. In her imagination, Malcolm was the one. He was her *knight in shining armor* that would whisk her away from life's problems. He had shown her what he wanted her to see. Malcolm would soon have to face his own problems. He would be her first. She took such pride in that thought.

"Well, baby girl, I am involved in some dangerous stuff. I have to do what I have to do. I want you to remember that. I kind of feel bad, but you know *you sought me out.*

Denise, looking confused said, "What in the world are you talking about?"

"You sought me out, remember, but you didn't know anything about me," stated Malcolm. Not totally convinced how this would all play out, Malcolm wanted to remind Denise of the facts.

"Your parents never told you about the streets and what could happen to you? People ain't what they pretend. People will use you and use you until they use you up. That's what my parents tried to tell me. Most days when you were coming home from school, I would be in the same spot, day after day, but you never noticed it. Didn't you think that was strange? I always had money, and my boys were always hanging around. Denise began to wonder at all that Malcolm was saying to her.

My Parents Tried

"My parents, they tried to steer me right, even took me to church on Sundays, but I was bad there, too. Soon no one wanted me around, so I created my own environment. Well, that's enough of that," he said.

Denise's faced was flushed with speculation as she said, "So what's up with the heart-felt confessions?" They both silently smirked at one another as the van kept on course to its secret destination.

I Warned You

Denise kept silent most of the ride. She was seriously thinking about what she heard between the mystery caller and Malcolm. Whatever Malcolm had been involved in, he now wanted out. What was it? What was the mysterious dealing that he attempted to confess about? Finally, they were at their destination.

Malcolm said to Denise, "Now, it's very important that you do just what I tell you to do, okay?"

"Okay."

"I need to get out and take care of some business with my boy, and then I'll be right back, and we will be on our way to a good time."

For the first time since leaving home, Denise began to feel a real sense of fear. She wished that someone she knew would drive by so she could excuse herself from such a dangerous situation. As Malcolm exited the van, Denise felt the urge to grab him and tell him to drive off, but there was nothing she could do. She sat still-faced as Malcolm walked around the back of the van and then out of sight. She could hear voices conversing back and forth, but she couldn't discern the words.

"Hey, what's up, Dog?"

"Everything is good," commented Malcolm.

The person stated, "So, you getting *cold feet* now? I thought things been going good for you since you been with us. Ain't we been taking care of you?"

"Well," said Malcolm, "all good things come to an end, and I am looking forward to moving on. I think I might have a good girl. She's from a good family. I've been watching her. She's still *wet behind the ears*, but she's trainable."

They both laughed. "Well," stated the visitor, "let's do our business and part our ways." Denise remained nervous as she sat in the waiting van, peering through the side mirror, looking for any indication of what was taking place behind the van.

Where's the Rest?

"Oh, oh, hold up! This ain't right. Now, Malcolm, you know what we discussed. This doesn't look good. Where's the rest?"

Malcolm, attempting to reason said, "Dog, we been doing business for sometime now, and you know I am good for it. I will make up the difference."

"Make up the difference! We don't do business like this, Malcolm. I am going to have to tell the man about this. Are you sure you don't have the rest?"

"Yes, I am sure," stated Malcolm. They parted ways and Malcolm rushed back to the van, and he and Denise suddenly drove off.

Denise and Malcolm never discussed what took place behind the van that day. Denise knew without asking that something wasn't right. She suspected it was about drugs, but she didn't know to what extent. Soon, however, Denise would find out. She was nervous the whole time they remained in the van.

What I Need Right Now

Somehow the recent experience with Malcolm jarred Denise in such a way as to cause her to long for home. She wanted to be home with her dad and Sheila. *Home had always been safe.* God was there. She missed the family dinners and nights out together. She thought, "What I need *right now* is in my book bag—my precious Bible and gospel music. Oh how I miss those jewels. I wonder whatever became of my book bag. If only I had those jewels with me now. Those precious messages on the blood, I need them now. I never thought I would long for them but oh, God, I need them now. I was wrong. I was wrong."

Denise never expected to be in this situation. She thought she was done with church and God. Denise tried her best to divorce herself from the rituals of her family, but now it was so funny. She found herself longing and yearning for those very things that she tried to get away from. You see, her Bible was in that book bag—a Bible that she had been given by her grandmother many years before. Why at one time, she would grab that engraved Bible and just look at it. It meant so much to her. During those turbulent times, she even slept with the Bible under her pillow. When she had taken a test and really wanted to pass, she went to the Psalms and recited the promises of God. Now things were different. Her book bag contained precious *little* books that seem so big. They were small excerpts of God's history, contained in little books that were "giant" in comfort, encouragement and direction. She had loved those books at one time. She felt that carrying them was like carrying around her grandmother's Bible, but in smaller form. At family prayer, she had her Bible. Denise took such pride in that Bible until she thought she had outgrown it. None of her friends even talked about reading the Bible. They made fun and criticized Denise when she spoke of her favorite passages. They didn't have to say a word as time went on because she put her Bible in her book bag and just left it there. Oh, what about those wonderful message tapes? She would mark "favorite" on a tape that she loved to listen to. At her church, the pastor had preached a series on home and family. She loved those tapes. She had played them over and over again, but now those favorites were hidden deep within her book bag. Denise needed to draw from the well that was within her book bag, but she had left it—left it behind.

Before I Could Get My Breath

"Is that her?"

"Grab her, quick, while no one is looking. We will keep her until Malcolm gives us what we want, or else."

As Denise left Z's house one afternoon, she was *abducted*, taken from her home. Before she could get fixed, the men had snatched Denise away in a waiting van and covered her mouth with a cloth soaked with some kind of chemical. She was beginning to go under. "Help! Help me Lord! …" Her voice was muzzled as she went unconscious. No one saw her. No one heard her. She was gone, whisked away.

4

MALCOLM'S CHOICE

Many Went Back

But there are some of you that believe not. For Jesus knew from the beginning who they were that believed not, and who should betray him. And he said, Therefore said I unto you, that no man can come unto me, except it were given unto him of my Father. From that *time* many of his disciples went back, and walked no more with him (John 6:64-66).

They Took Me to Church

"*My parents tried to steer me right, even took me to church on Sundays, but I always acted out and soon no one wanted me around, so I created my own environment,*" Malcolm remembered from his last conversation with Denise. It was nearly time for the sun to come bursting forth. "It will be good to *start over*, to get my life right," he reflected before opening his eyes to a brand new day. Growing weary with a life of drugs and abuse, Malcolm wanted to make a new choice, a different choice. Malcolm wanted to start making the right choices in his life.

Gang Initiation

Malcolm had survived it all—the gang initiation and the gang life. He had witnessed the price paid by many of his friends vying to get into the gang. Once, a potential member carried a razor blade inside a mall and searched for a victim to slice. It was his initiation examination to be invited into the gang.

On another instance, Malcolm heard of one potential member jumping in the back of a parked car one evening. When discovered by the police, the boy indicated that he was joining a gang and the initiation was to kidnap a young girl and rape her. The captured young boy was later taken to prison on kidnapping charges. Malcolm continued pondering in his mind, "Why did I even allow things to get this far? How did I even get started in all of this?"

Always a Follower

Malcolm had always been a follower. He was never able to excel in school, having been demoted once in grammar school. He never finished high school. Hanging out with the local crowd was so easy. It required no effort, no self-esteem, and no *fight*.

Like many of our youth today, Malcolm had escaped into a *false sense of security* by pretending to be someone that he was not. In an effort to escape life's troubles, many youth join a gang, kill someone or become influenced by drugs. Like Malcolm, many of today's youth are struggling with *something*. It may be a drug-addicted parent, molestation, or a poor academic life. *Suffering is no excuse to surrender your life to the enemy.* There is enough fight in you to make it—to survive.

Don't look at those who are failing or hanging with the *in-crowd*. Seek to be like those who have *made it* in life. In your environment, there may not be many people *but there is someone* that can inspire you to do well and make good choices in your life. Look for that individual. No matter what others are doing, you can make the difference with your life. You have to decide that you are worth fighting for. You are worth so much to God but you must contend to find *your* place. You won't find that place without first knowing who you are.

Dare To Be Different

Dare to be different! God will stand by your side. His word promises it. **I will never leave thee, nor forsake thee** (Hebrews 13:5). The Lord has promised you constant companionship. **When my father and my mother forsake me, then the Lord will take me up** (Psalm 27:10). This is your promise from God. He will stay with you as long as you will stay with Him. He seeks to be your guide, leader, comforter, friend, and Saviour.

Malcolm passed up many opportunities to improve in school. His parents went through great lengths to obtain all the help necessary to assist Malcolm, but he rebelled and was kicked out of each and every program. Having exhausted all their efforts and finances, Malcolm's parents *let him go*. "Malcolm you're getting too old. It's time to get yourself together. One day, you will look back on these times and regret many of the decisions that you have made. You must make good choices, choices that will prove beneficial in your life," said his parents. Malcolm's parents knew all too well the adage of "living with the decisions you make."

Malcolm's Rebellion

It seemed that Malcolm's rebellion increased with each and every attempt to help him in school, church, or society. *He wanted what he wanted*. Malcolm made bad choices early in his life, thinking he would have so much time to make things right. Malcolm underestimated life and thought that he could afford to make wrong choices in his youth, and then, *when he was ready*, he could chose to do right. But Malcolm learned that life isn't like that. Life demonstrated cruelty beyond the likes of anything that Malcolm had ever experienced. *Only* then did he *fully* understand.

Malcolm had witnessed much violence during his gang-life. He saw one of his best friends killed, execution style, for failing to kill a rival gang member.

Settle Down

"Today, I am going to *start my life over again*," thought Malcolm as his feet hit the floor. He would put the gang life far behind him. Malcolm looked forward to settling down. It would be such a relief not to always be looking over his shoulder. His thoughts of leaving the gang lifestyle were very naïve.

Malcolm foolishly thought that he could just walk away from his gang life. How quickly he forgot his last conversation with the man he met behind the van. He would do things differently—make different choices than he had made in the past. Malcolm was anxious to tell Denise.

He hurried to get himself ready to meet Denise, but then an eerie feeling suddenly took hold of him. He couldn't put his finger on it, but the feeling made him afraid. He felt nervous and wanted to talk to someone. Malcolm reached for his cell phone to call Denise. He made several attempts, but each time he was immediately connected to her voicemail. "Man, what's up with that?" thought Malcolm. He placed his cell phone down and continued preparing for the day with a sense of trepidation.

Something Was Wrong

No matter what Malcolm attempted to do, that strange, fearful feeling would not leave him alone. Several minutes later, he attempted to contact Denise again. He had never called her home because he had always been able to reach Denise through her cell phone. This time was different, and Malcolm knew it. Something was very wrong. He sat on the sofa and attempted to put his suspicious feelings in perspective.

Where's Denise?

"Ok, Denise, where are you?" questioned Malcolm. "Now wouldn't that be something? I'll go through all this stuff, give up dealing, change my life, and have this girl go off and do something stupid like try and be with somebody else," pondered Malcolm. That old feeling of failure plagued him just as it had in grammar school. He never felt able to really achieve and barely made the grade. Was that the case here? Did Malcolm risk his relationship with Denise by taking her with him to do his last deal? "Just like everything else in my life, I've probably failed at this, too. She probably thinks I am some drug-dealing, drug-tooting fool but I'm not. I'm not. She's the reason why I want to change," thought Malcolm.

Had this all been a big mistake? Malcolm, in a panic raced again for his cell phone and dialed Denise's number over and over again. He kept getting the voice mail. In a frantic effort to reach Denise, he called her aunt's house. Malcolm dialed the number. The phone rung. Someone picked up the receiver, and Malcolm immediately blurted out, "Hello Z, my name is Malcolm. I don't know if Denise has told you about me, but I've been trying to reach her this morning, and I can't seem to find her. Have you seen her? Is she there with you?"

There was a long pause as Malcolm waited for a response. He couldn't refrain himself and shouted, "Hello, hello, are you there?"

Just as Z started to speak, Malcolm's cell phone beeped to let him know that there was another caller waiting on the other line.

Who's on the Other End?

Malcolm, nearly out of breath, cut off Denise's aunt and switched to the other line. "Hello, hello, hello," shouted Malcolm but there was no response from the caller. There was just breathing, breathing. The caller didn't identify himself, but, after a few short seconds, hung up the telephone. Malcolm attempted to redial the number without success. He sat on the sofa in a dazed-like state. Suddenly, his telephone rung again, and the caller refused to identify himself, but simply sighed into the receiver. Malcolm had forgotten all about Denise's aunt. He was nearly hysterical.

His telephone rung a few minutes later. It was Z. "Hello, Malcolm," stated Z.

"Yes, it's me," Malcolm replied.

"Now what's this all about regarding Denise? She isn't there? I haven't seen her since last night when you picked her up in some van you were driving. What in the world is going on between you two?" asked Z.

What Do We Do Now?

"So what's the plan, Dog?" shouted a voice.

"Just be quiet, and do what I say. I will tell you what you need to know, when you need to know it and not before then," Dog replied.

"Dog, what we gone do now? We can't keep riding around with her like this. She's been out for sometime now. How do we know the stuff that we gave her didn't harm her?"

"Oh, now you're religious? Shut that hole in your face or I'll ... I need to send a message to Malcolm. He crossed me, and people don't cross me and live," Dog said.

Denise lay unconscious as the two men continued to drive to some unknown destination. She laid flat on the van floor with her mouth muzzled. Suddenly, out of nowhere, sirens started going off behind them.

"What is going on?" Dog, we gon' get caught. We gon' get life, ain't we?"

"Slow down and pull over. Don't freak out, or they will suspect something. Remember, if I go down, I will blame all this on you. So play it calm and cool. You got me?"

"Yeah, Dog, I hear ya."

Pull Over

"Pull over to the right. Pull over to the right," sternly echoed a voice from behind their van. "Step out of the vehicle and put your hands where we can see them," stated one of the two officers.

"Good morning officer, what seems to be the problem?" asked one of the men. "Where's your proof of insurance and registration? Get it," shouted the other officer.

The two policemen stood about six feet tall, and their voices would make anyone tremble. The officers checked the insurance and registration, and then one of the officers asked, "Where are you two going, and what is the van going to be used for?"

"Officer, we use this van to carry music equipment, and that's it. Did we do something wrong?"

One officer stated, "We've been trailing you for a while now, and something just didn't seem quite right, so we decided to pull you two over. Get in the van and get going. Don't let me see either one of you out here anymore today."

They rushed back to the van and sped off.

Give Her Some More Stuff

Denise seemed to be coming to. She was moaning and groaning, twisting herself on the van floor. "Get her. Give her some more stuff. She must stay still until we get to where we're going, and then we'll call Malcolm and see if he's ready to do business," Dog said.

"Okay, Dog."

They drove a few more miles and came to an abandoned apartment building. The owner lived across town, and the men thought it would be safe to hold Denise up there. The apartment had been vacated for sometime, and the building was damp and cold. There were mouse droppings all over the place. "Quick, grab her, and bring her inside," Dog said.

"Uh, can you help me? She ain't a little girl." One grabbed her head and shoulders, and the other grabbed her legs. They rushed her inside one of the empty apartments and threw her on the floor. The shuffle bruised Denise. While unconscious, she moaned and groaned for some time.

Hey Malcolm, Missing Something?

After adjusting Denise and getting themselves comfortable, a cell phone emerged from one of the men's pockets and one of them dialed Malcolm's number. Malcolm's cell phone rung. "Hello, hello," shouted Malcolm.

"Malcolm, it's me. You got the rest of my money?" Dog asked.

"Dog, is this you? What's up man? I told you that I would settle up with you," Malcolm said.

"Malcolm, when you gon' have my stuff, man?" Dog shouted.

"Soon," stated Malcolm, "Real, real soon."

Dog asked, "Hey Malcolm, *missing something*?" and hung up the telephone.

Malcolm realized, "My God, they have Denise!" He dropped to the floor and held his head in his hands in total disbelief.

5

A LONG WAY FROM HOME

Lessons Learned

Have you ever been homesick? Have you ever experienced that *longing, aching* feeling that grips the inner most chamber of your stomach as you yearn for the presence of family and friends—those who know you best? Life is full of surprises, and it comes packed with *lessons learned*. At times, life can be a real *tough* schoolmaster.

Sound the Alarm

Mom and Dad sound the alarm and shout the warnings of life into your head, but some will never take heed. Life then becomes the *cruel* taskmaster. While living at home, life seems hard, and parents appear to be more like tyrants than parents. *Someone's always telling you what to do*, treating you like a baby. "Don't they know that I am grown—well almost?" This sentiment is echoed by many of our youth today. There's an eagerness to be free of the constraints and confinement of home, but be very careful. I am sure the prodigal son felt the same way, but later he discovered that he had been deceived. ***Deceit*** is the act or practice of concealing or distorting the truth for the purpose of misleading.

And he said, A certain man had two sons: And the younger of them said to his father, Father, give me the portion of goods that falleth to me. And he divided unto them his living. And not many days after the younger son gathered all together, and took his journey into a far country, and there wasted his substance with riotous living. *And when he had spent all*, there arose a mighty famine in that land; and he began to be in want. And he went and joined himself to a citizen of that country; and he sent him into his fields to feed swine. And he would fain have filled his belly with the husks that the swine did eat: and no man gave unto him (Luke 15:11-16).

***And when he came to himself*, he said, How many hired servants of my father's have bread enough and to spare, and I perish with hunger! I will arise and go to my father, and will say unto him, Father, I have sinned against heaven, and before thee, And am no more worthy to be called thy son: make me as one of thy hired servants. And he arose, and came to his father. But when he was yet a great way off, his father saw him, and had compassion, and ran, and fell on his neck, and kissed him** (Luke 15:17-20).

The prodigal son came to himself and returned home, but you might not have the time that he had. Feeding swine is nothing in comparison to what life can thrust you into.

To Go the Other Way

Like the prodigal son, Denise didn't carefully consider all that was ahead of her. How could she? She had been protected and sheltered from much of life's danger. Her father and mother had put forth a great effort in attempting to shield Denise, but they could only do so much for a daughter who had her mind made up to go the other way. There are many "Denises" in the world today. The enemy has convinced many of our sons and daughters that any place is better than home, but they will learn just as Denise *had to learn*. Many won't learn *until it is too late*. When sin is done with you, then what? When you have fulfilled the lust of the flesh and the lust of the eyes, then what? When sin has robbed you of eternal life, then what? Only you have the answer. **For all that is in the world, the lust of the flesh, and the lust of the eyes, and the pride of life, is not of the Father, but is of the world** (I John 2:16).

Her Plan, Her Way

Her plan was well thought out, or so she believed. **There is a way that seemeth right unto a man; but the end thereof are the ways of death** (Proverbs 16:25).

Denise presumed to have it all figured out. Remember her last night at home during Thanksgiving? She thought, "I can't wait until I am grown. I want to get out of this house and do my own thing. I won't have to listen to anyone. I want to be my own person." Remember how she had been discontented and how she began to dread the time in the church services? Notice the pattern. There is a pattern to each person's life. You don't just *fall out of love* with God and His divine plan for your life. There are definite steps taken. A person doesn't *fall* into sin; it is often a step-by-step process. Many times people have left God *long before* physically exiting the church door.

So Intoxicated

Denise had been so intoxicated with the idea of *being on her own*. She once stated, "I am going to leave my mark on this world. I'll show them all that I can take care of myself." But now things were different. Life didn't flow like Denise thought it would. Blinded by her desires, Denise allowed her vision to be blurred by television. She held onto the fabricated tales of others, but Denise was in the *real* world now.

Malcolm and His Wife

"Malcolm, come on. Mom and Dad will be waiting," stated Denise to her husband, Malcolm.

"Just one minute, let me grab the kids. You know we can't leave them behind," replied Malcolm. Malcolm and his wife, Denise, were all packed up and ready for a nice Sunday dinner at Sheila and William's house. They always went there, each Sunday, after Sunday service for some down-home cookin.' Denise and Malcolm hadn't missed a meal since they were married, several years earlier.

"Boy," stated Malcolm, "I don't know where we would be if your parents had not let us stay with them while we both finished school."

"You're right," stated Denise, "I don't know what we would have done. I am so glad that we waited and listened to my parents. Their advice didn't make a whole lot of sense at the time but I'm sure glad we listened."

I Am Glad

"You know, we haven't missed one thing," Malcolm said and started laughing. "You know, Denise, we were in such a rush to get on our own. Boy, we fought your parents tooth and nail, but I am glad they didn't yield to our demands and let us have our way. We would have been quite the couple, with no formal education and no way to take care of ourselves, and with children, that would have been a mess—we would have a hot mess."

I Was Wrong

As they were pulling into Denise's parent's driveway, she stated, "Boy, the devil will really pull one over on you if you aren't careful. Just think—all the times I sat and thought about leaving home, running away even, all the times I thought about how cruel and mean my parents were. I honestly thought they were crazy and had forgotten about what it was like to live—forgotten what it was like to be young—but I was wrong. I was all wrong. We have such a happy life now."

As they exited the van and approached Denise's parent's house, Shelia said, "Hello Denise and Malcolm. Where are my road dogs?" "Road dog" was the name she had given to Denise and Malcolm's twins. She dragged them all over town, and they happily managed to keep up somehow. Sheila and William had so much fun with their grandchildren.

"Hey, Grandma!" one of the twins shouted as they both raced to be the first to reach Grandma's arms for the beginning of many hugs of the evening. Life was good, real good.

Just a Dream

Feeling as if she had been thrown from a truck, Denise struggled to regain consciousness as she lay amidst the dust, filth, and darkness on what seemed to be an abandoned apartment floor. She didn't know where she was. "Dream. Dream. I was dreaming of home," Denise soberly thought. "I am not married. My parents aren't on the porch waiting for my kids to run to them. It has all been a dream. Malcolm is not my husband. He's not even here now," reflected Denise. Denise had been dreaming, dreaming of how she wanted life to be. Maybe she began to have such fantasies in an effort ***to escape the harsh reality*** of her life.

Bam!

Denise's body was racking with pain. She felt the need to regurgitate. Her stomach was eager to relieve itself. Denise had been pumped with an enormous amount of drugs, and now she was feeling the aftermath of it all. Her head started spinning, and all she could do was pass out. Bam! Her body hit the cold, dusty floor. She was out—again.

"What am I going to do? They have Denise. How can I explain this to her parents? Oh my God! Denise! Denise!" howled Malcolm. What would he do? He thought he could go to the devil's gambling table without penalty, but life isn't like that, is it?

Be not deceived; God is not mocked: for *whatsoever* a man soweth, that shall he also reap (Galatians 6:7). **For he that soweth to his flesh shall of the flesh reap corruption; but he that soweth to the Spirit shall of the Spirit reap life everlasting** (Galatians 6:8).

Malcolm's Choice

Malcolm's choice was to leave the gang life behind. He was done with it all, but Malcolm didn't realize that there was a price. He thought that he could *play* and leave the *game* when he wanted, but that is not what happened. Malcolm had been exposed. His secret was out, and Malcolm had to face his demons and Denise's parents. There was no way he could hide it under a rug. He couldn't conceal himself behind a façade and pretend to be mighty and strong. When Malcolm was growing up, he made everyone laugh—he was the class clown—but now life was playing a cruel joke on Malcolm. Life was cackling at his sudden dilemma. He would be forced to confront the choices made earlier in his life.

Full Circle

Malcolm's life had come *full circle*. All the lessons he should have learned, where were they now? Life had visited Malcolm with the sting of hurt, fear and uncertainty. What would he do? He couldn't lie. Denise's parents were sure to find out that their daughter was missing. Had it all been worth it—the stealing and gang bangin'? Malcolm was the one left holding the bag. The only way out of this *almost impossible* situation was to face the truth—***no more lies***.

Just like Malcolm, you will experience a time when you must face yourself with all deceit gone. No matter. What will you do? Look at the price Malcolm may be forced to render for *the years he enjoyed in sin*. In his youth, there was gang bangin' women, drugs, robbery, and being disobedient to his parents. He lived his life in the *fast lane*, but now the hand of time was turning against Malcolm. Was it too little, too late?

I Won't Deny Thee

Peter answered and said unto him, Though all men shall be offended because of thee, yet will I never be offended. Jesus said unto him, Verily I say unto thee, That this night, before the cock crow, thou shalt deny me thrice. Peter said unto him, Though I should die with thee, yet will I not deny thee. Likewise also said all the disciples (Matthew 26:33-35).

A Lot of Mouth

Peter had a lot of mouth. He was impulsive by nature and childish. Peter wanted what he wanted when he wanted it. Peter did a lot of talking, never realizing that one day he would be forced to give an account of his beliefs. Peter was unable to stand in the moment of crisis. Jesus attempted, on several occasions, to get Peter ready but he was *always* in and out, up and down. Jesus' plan and mission never became a reality to Peter before Pentecost. He was simply *"playin' church—going through the motions—simply having a form."* Is that you?

I Don't Know the Man!

Now Peter sat without in the palace: and a damsel came unto him, saying, Thou also wast with Jesus of Galilee. But he denied before them all, saying, I know not what thou sayest. And when he was gone out into the porch, another maid saw him, and said unto them that were there, This fellow was also with Jesus of Nazareth. And again he denied with an oath, I do not know the man. And after a while came unto him they that stood by, and said to Peter, Surely thou also art one of them; for thy speech bewrayeth thee. Then began he to curse and to swear, saying, I know not the man. And immediately the cock crew. And Peter remembered the word of Jesus, which said unto him, Before the cock crow, thou shalt deny me thrice. And he went out, and wept bitterly (Matthew 26:69-75).

Peter Had To Curse

Peter's life had been studied by others. He could not hide the fact that he had been with Jesus. Now Peter's life came crashing in on him. He never thought that Jesus would leave him. With strong words, he denied ever knowing the Christ. Peter had to curse to persuade others that *he was not of* Christ, and at that point, he was no longer of Christ. Later, after his conversion, Peter would travel as a missionary and his ministry would be long and fruitful. Many would come to know the Lord because of Peter's Spirit-filled teachings. With such sober reality, historians have recorded that at his crucifixion, Peter chose to be killed upside down, not considering himself worthy to be sacrificed like his Master was.

Peter spoke a foreign language. He no longer spoke the love language — the language that he had once witnessed which delivered so many. Peter was there as Jesus delivered so many with the love language, but now he was different. Peter was following afar off. The Holy Ghost, the Spirit of Truth, He is the only one who has the power to bridge such a gap. He and He alone is the one who can close up the spaces and fill in the gaps as a result of hurt feelings and disappointments.

Peter had been lukewarm, following so far behind and warming his hands with the enemy — joining those who would crucify Christ. **And they that had laid hold on Jesus led him away to Caiaphas the high priest, where the scribes and the elders were assembled. But Peter followed him afar off unto the high priest's palace, and went in, and sat with the servants, to see the end** (Matthew 26:57-58).

The Love of God

And the Lord turned, and looked upon Peter. And Peter remembered the word of the Lord, how he had said unto him, Before the cock crow, thou shalt deny me thrice. And Peter went out and wept bitterly (Luke 22:61, 62). Peter once witnessed and handled the power of God but now he followed afar off. This night, he remembered the words of Jesus; the words that could have tormented him for the rest of his life ... *"Thou shalt deny me."* How would Peter ever recover from such a failure? Would he ever be able to lift his head again from such shame?

Peter repented, was forgiven, and went on to become a great, great vessel for the Lord in the beginning of the Church. He, however, had to make a choice--*live in the past*, or *go on into the greatness of God*. Go on yielding in the love of God to never make the same mistake again. Peter, no doubt, always regretted having failed the Lord, but after he was forgiven, he had no condemnation. *Peter had to face facts about his failure and realize that he couldn't go back and undo his betrayal.* Instead, he chose to be thankful for having had another chance to show forth God's greatness to others. Peter chose to press forward; to be all he could be for the kingdom of God. He chose to rise up — up above his terrible disappointment to God.

But Peter, standing up with the eleven, lifted up his voice, and said unto them. Ye men of Judaea, and all ye that dwell at Jerusalem, be this known unto you, and hearken to my words: For these are not drunken, as ye suppose, seeing it is but the third hour of the day. *But this is that which was spoken by the prophet Joel; And it shall come to pass in the last days, saith God, I will pour out of my Spirit upon all flesh* (Acts 2:14-117a).

A Sober Mind

With all deceit gone, Malcolm knew that he must contact Denise's parents. His heart raced faster than at any other time in his life, except for when he almost overdosed due to ingesting too many drugs. This was the only time in his adult life that Malcolm was up all night and unable to sleep. The sound of his heart was so boisterous that it seemed as if his heart was outside of his body, not inside. Malcolm's heart raced with fear and trepidation. Surely this thing would cost him his life, either by murder or by shear dread, *but he wasn't dead yet.* That would be too easy. No, he would live. Malcolm had to live. *He had to live so he could learn.*

Looking for a Way Out

How often, when faced with what seems to be an insurmountable problem, do you start looking for a *way out?* Why do you think gang membership is so high? It's a *false* family—a *false* safe haven—because it promises something that only the truth can bring—real love. Anything else will not last. No matter how good it looks, how good it feels at the time, it will not last. *Only real love will last.* Only real love will cure all that is going on with you and in you. Only real love will heal *all* past hurts, past failures, and past disappointments. You must choose love in order for love to work for you. No matter if your parents' failed you—no matter who abandoned you or disappointed you in your childhood, love will heal. Love will heal! **For God *so* loved the world that he gave his only begotten Son, That whosoever believeth in him should not perish, but have everlasting life** (John 3:16).

Those of you who have left God, why not return? Return to your first love. He will be there to guide and keep you. He will show you the way back to His love, back to Calvary. His road is blood-covered and blood-anointed. His road is paved with righteousness and holiness. Daily, He is offering you all of Himself for this, your last and final journey. His grace, goodness, and mercy are all reaching your way, through the Holy Spirit, bidding you come home while there is yet time. This love call—this great dispensation of God's longing and reaching for man will soon end. If you have left your first love, you must go back, yes, **go back to the beginning**. Remember? It was so easy for you to leave all for the sake of Christ. You were so compelled to His mission and vision of reaching lost humanity. Love requires work and effort on each part. Whatever you did in the beginning, you must do the same to remain faithful. You must regain the vision of reaching lost humanity. Nothing else matters.

Mending Bridges

"I must do it. I have to do this right now," reasoned Malcolm. "What will Denise's parents say? I am sure that they will be full of anger. I must finish this. I must make things right, no matter the cost to myself. Others are involved, and it's my responsibility to fix things," said Malcolm. He reached for the telephone and attempted to dial the numbers. His mind went blank. He struggled to keep his hand steady as he dialed the numbers. Finally the telephone rang. "Hello," Malcolm uttered.

Sheila said, "Who is this?"

Malcolm attempted to remain calm and said, "Hello, my name is Malcolm. I am not sure if you know me or not, but I am dating your daughter, Denise."

"Hello there, Malcolm, and how is my daughter these days?" questioned Sheila.

You Could Hear a Pin Drop

Malcolm's whole body seemed as if it would cave in and shut down at any moment. The air was still, and you could hear a pin drop. Malcolm's heartbeat was getting louder and louder as he forced himself to say, "Well, that's why I'm calling. I haven't had any contact with Denise in a couple of days, but I have an idea where she may be."

"Well, out with it boy, where is Denise? Did she put you up to this? She's always up to something. Why, I remember this one time," joked Sheila, "she got so mad at us that she decided that she was leaving home. Denise packed up some stuff in her book bag and ended up going nowhere. So what's this all about, Malcolm?"

"There's been a small problem," Malcolm said.

Sheila's voice sharply and abruptly changed. She asked, "What kind of problem? Hold on—hold on son. Let me get Denise's dad on the other line. William, there's some young man on the telephone who says he's dating Denise and something about a problem. William, are you there? Please pick up the receiver!"

It took William just a moment to grab the telephone, but to Malcolm, who waited, hoping for the next breath to come, it seemed like an eternity. "Hello, this is Denise's father. And who did you say you were?" asked William. There was a long pause. "Hello. Hello," pressed William. "Sheila, who is that on the telephone?" Malcolm took a deep breath and said, "Hi, my name is Malcolm, and I am dating your daughter."

When Malcolm opened his mouth to form the next words, his telephone made a clicking sound, indicating that there was another caller waiting to reach him. Malcolm, full of fear and scared to death, dropped the telephone. Suddenly, all connection was lost to both Denise's parents and the other caller who was waiting to get through. "Hello. Hello. Hello." were echoed voices as the receiver fell to the floor.

Shut Up

"What was that, Dog? Maybe we didn't dial the right number," said the caller.

"Oh, shut up. Don't you think I know Malcolm's number? Give me the phone."

"I'll try again," concluded the caller. "Don't snatch, Dog."

Sit Down and Be Quiet

"William," pressed Sheila.

"Sheila, sit down and be quiet," sternly replied William. "We don't know that there is anything wrong. You know how you get, so cool it!"

In actuality, both William and Sheila were quite upset by now. They couldn't even return the call to Malcolm because the number was protected and didn't show up on caller identification. "I knew something like this might happen, William," continued Sheila.

"Sheila, go take a pill or something. You are making my head pound," replied William. "He will call again. I promise you."

William truly prayed that Malcolm would contact them again. William's mind went back—way back to the day that Denise left the home. The scene played over and over in his mind. The pain resurfaced—the wound was ripped opened once again.

Remember When?

William's mind was lost—lost in the memories and emotions of that day. William shook himself and attempted to regain some type of composure. He felt himself being sucked back—back into that horrible, horrible moment when his baby girl left home.

Denise Heard Voices

There was a cool draft, which hovered over Denise. In fact, it broke her sleep. Nauseated and weakened by all of the drugs given her, Denise heard voices coming from another room, not too far away. She continued trying to make some sense out of the place she was in. It was dark, and mouse droppings covered most of the empty space. Denise could sense that the entire building had been abandoned for some time.

Her attention was drawn toward the voices. She heard Malcolm's name and sat up straight. "What exactly is going on?" Denise wondered. "Who are these people? Why am I here? And why are they talking about Malcolm?" She listened with intensity as she tried to make sense out of her life these last few days. Denise could not refrain from thinking about her mother and father. She loved them dearly, and she now realized that she needed them more than ever before. Denise longed for the company of her parents. If she could only call one of them, certainly they would make everything all right. No matter how old she got, she would always be daddy's little girl.

I Need My Book Bag!

Oh, how Denise ached from deep down inside for the comfort of home— the comfort of safety. She missed her church family and all the outings, skits, and plays. Denise thought of all the valuable information that she pushed away into her book bag. Surely, some reference hidden there would help her in this situation, but she had abandoned her book bag. She had told Sharon that she wouldn't ever need that book bag again, but Denise had been mistaken. She had been deceived. Denise was not as grown as she pretended to be. Life was just as Mom and Dad tried to tell her—and now look—she was in a dark place with strangers and all alone.

As she reminisced about home, a small rodent shot across the floor and flew straight up the sleeve of her torn shirt. Afraid of being exposed and given more drugs, Denise simply shook the mouse out of her sleeve and flung it across the room. The rodent incident seemed so small in comparison to missing home. Denise then grabbed herself and just began to rock back and forth.

She Was Praying

She didn't realize it at the time, but she was praying, praying to God. She knew how to pray. Denise never felt the need for prayer before, but she knew—yes, she knew how to pray. From within, she cried unto the only one who could help her at the time. She cried with such longing, such godly sorrow, such sincerity and such shame. Denise had been fooled. The memory of the church services started to overwhelm her. Before her mind could complete one thought of one day, instantly another thought would flood her mind, and on and on it went for what seemed like hours. Actually, it was just a few minutes. Denise, for the first time, realized that she was *a long way from home* with no one to help her. Who would she blame? *She alone* was to blame. The emptiness that shadowed Denise brought new insight into just how far into deceit she had fallen. She had been blindsided. That's the way deceit works. You don't know how far off you are until you are in grave trouble. When you are blindsided, you can't see that something or someone that is so close to you. You may not see the devices of the enemy being manifested in their lives. The fragments of deceit may be so small that without the guiding and leading of the Holy Spirit, they will remain undetected until too late. You have to turn completely around to view all the opposition—turn completely around with all deceit gone, using the light of God's truth for every life.

Those whom you follow, those individuals that have influence in your life, do you truly know them? They may be your brothers, sisters, mother, or father. We must not be weary in well doing; we will reap, reap, and reap if we faint not. God is faithful. No matter what the Lord does for some, they'll never, never know the hour that they are in. Many of us don't realize the limited time that we have. We don't realize how close to the brink of hell some of our close kin are, or we would be screaming for them now. Take heed. It's time to put things aside.

We have been brought to the kingdom for such an hour as this. We must remember that God chose us—we didn't choose Him.

Where Are the Friends?

Where were the friends now? There was no party to go to. No, all she wanted to do was lie in Mom's bed and review the day. At one time, Denise thought she was too grown to lie in Momma's bed but this day—today, she longed for home—home. She seemed to have second thoughts now—second thoughts about her existence and, yes, her purpose. God had truly been with her all of her life, but Denise didn't realize it until now. From her innermost being and probably for the first time, she cried out to God. Guess what? God was listening.

Oh, God

Denise parted her lips and began to whisper, "Oh, God. I am so, so, so sorry for all of the pain. I thank you, Lord, for this day, a day that I've taken for granted for most of my life. I don't even know if you can help me now. When you beckoned for me to come and spend time with you—pray and read your word—I didn't have time, but please help me. I am so very weak, and I don't know what these men plan to do with me. I don't want to die. I want to live. I want to live. I want to live and serve you."

Get Malcolm Back on the Phone

"Get Malcolm back on the phone now … you idiot," screamed one of the men.

"Malcolm, no more games. Do you have my stuff or what? Don't make me do something that you will be sorry about for the rest of your life," concluded the caller. He didn't wait to see if Malcolm was the one picking up the phone. He just shouted his message and, when done, slammed down the phone.

"Hey boss, what was that all about?" the man asked the other.

"Oh, shut up. You are starting to get on my nerves. Come on, let's go," the man shouted.

"Hey, you are always shouting. Where we going anyway?"

Now Wait a Minute

They both walked toward a closed door which was not locked. "Hey, how many times have I told you to keep this door locked? You don't have the brains of a fly," yelled a man. They both proceeded to a van just outside the unlocked door. The trunk was partially opened.

"Oh man, didn't I tell you to lock this trunk?" the man insisted.

"Now, wait one minute. I know that I locked the door and this trunk. I ain't gon' let you keep blaming me for all this stuff," the man shouted to his angry friend.

Did You Really?

"So, where are we going?" asked one of the men.

"Can you make sure that everything is locked up? If we didn't have Denise drugged up, she could easily get away … because of YOU!"

"G, what's up with the screaming? She's still lying on that floor. I gave her enough stuff to keep her out for a long, long time," said the man. "Did you really? Go and check on her. I have to look after you like a little child. Hey. Hey, never mind, let's go. I need to pick up some stuff. I guess Malcolm needs a special delivery. If that is the way that he wants to play, then that's the way we will play it," smirked the caller. They both jumped into the van after slamming the trunk shut.

Pull Over

Not ten minutes after leaving, they heard a sound. "What in the world is that? Say, Idiot, did you close the trunk?"

"Of course. You talk to me like I am stupid. Well, I ain't stupid, Dog!"

A loud siren pierced out the words, "Pull over. Pull over. Pull over now." The van immediately pulled over to the right of the street. Both men emerged from the van and met the officers. "Hey, back in the van. No one told you to get out. Get back in the van. Where is your proof of insurance and registration?" the officer demanded.

"Okay officer, just one minute," the man said. "Here you are officer."

The officer reviewed the credentials and asked, "Do you know why I stopped you?"

Call the police

Sheila was truly a basket case, by this time. Several hours had passed with no return call from Malcolm. "William, should we call the police?" cried Sheila.

"Sheila, Malcolm never eluded that Denise was in trouble. Just sit down and wait. If we don't hear anything in the next few hours, then we will call the police. We don't know much about Malcolm. Do you know where he lives? Sheila, do you know where he works? Does he even have a job?" questioned William.

Oh God

"Oh God, please help me. I need you to help me this time. I have no one else to turn to. I couldn't live with the fact that something happened to Denise because of my sins," cried Malcolm.

He thought, "What in the world are they going to do to Denise? He didn't even give me a chance to respond. Oh, please don't hurt Denise. I wish I knew where they took her. Maybe I ought to call the police. Yes, that's what I will do, but first I will have to tell Denise's parents all that has happened." Malcolm knew he would have to make things right—right with God.

Beverly Denise Thomas

The Holy Spirit has everything to do with the conversion. He brings us into the knowledge of our sin against God's holy word. He continues to deal with us, and we are drawn to God's truth that if we don't repent, we'll never see His face. Through the truth brought to us by the precious Holy Spirit, we are convicted of our sins, and we beg for mercy—and we get it. It is so easy for God to forgive a heart that comes full of godly sorrow—so, so sorry for treading the precious blood of Jesus Christ under foot. So sorry for making the Holy Spirit cry. So sorry for crucifying Jesus afresh. There in our brokenness, we find mercy, grace, restoration, and regeneration. This is what awaited Malcolm. He was ready. Finally, he was ready.

Open the Trunk

"How long has your back light been out?" the policeman asked.

"Officer," said the man, "I didn't know there was a problem. I will have it looked at right away."

The officer walked around to the back of the van and bent down to see if he could see into the trunk and walked back to the driver's side and asked, "Got anything in the trunk?"

"No, Officer, there is nothing in the trunk," said one of the men.

"Maybe I should have a look anyway," stated the officer.

"Officer, let me get my keys, and I will open the trunk for you." Convinced that they had nothing hidden, the officer gave them a warning and let them go on their way.

How Did the Light Get Broken?

They questioned one another about how the back light could have been broken. They arrived at a local hardware store, purchased some items, and returned the van only to find that the trunk was left opened once again. They each looked with fear into the eyes of the other and jumped in the van and raced back to the abandoned apartment building. Without saying one word to the other, they both knew what the other was thinking—the last few hours, the door being left unlocked, the trunk left unlocked, the back light broken and finally, being stopped by the cops. Something wasn't adding up.

They exited the half-parked van and ran into the apartment building. They raced to the place where *they thought* they had left Denise. It was like the last few miles of a long, long race, with the finish line in view. One man ran and pushed the other man, who then fell to the floor with both eyes focused toward the room where Denise had been held captive. The other man, panting, full of fear, anxious, and now flushed with anger, pushed through the door and ran toward what ***seemed*** to be a body covered by a worn, dust-filled blanket. As he swiftly threw the blanket back, his mind raced with the possibilities of imprisonment and even the charge of murder. The cover came unpeeled in his hands, as it moved at the horrified man's forceful command. His eyes stared down toward the image. The other man still lay fearfully on the floor, near the entrance. The man on the floor knew that bad or good would be determined by the next words from that room.

    She was gone!

6

FULL CIRCLE

Without Walls Ministry

It was "Youth Day" at *Without Walls Ministry*, and people were pressing their way to get in and get a seat. Youth day was always popular at the church where William and Sheila Whiting had been members for years. Why, they hadn't missed a service in several years—only that one time, when William had suffered the tragic loss of his close friend, Brice. Other than that, they were committed and faithful members. "Good morning William and Sheila," shouted one of the members as they exited their vehicle.

"Good morning to you both," replied William. "It's good to be here, isn't it?" asked William.

"Yes," commented the couple, almost simultaneously. They all rushed into the cool building. It was about eighty-five degrees outside on that wonderful summer day. The music ministry had concluded, and the collection had been taken. All eyes gazed toward the front, as the ushers retrieved more chairs from the back to accommodate guests.

The pastor, Reverend Breen, got up to announce the Youth Day speaker. "Good morning, everyone, and happy Youth Day. I am always excited to do the introductions on Youth Day. With so many of our youth leaving the Lord, it is good to see those returning and those remaining faithful to the cause. Can I get an amen?"

The entire church unanimously exploded with, "AMEN!"

"We have heard this young lady many times before, and her story never grows old. Well, let me move on out the way. Everyone standing. That means you, too, Caleb. You ain't too old for me to get you, boy," laughed Rev. Breen. "That boy. That's my boy. He's with the pros now. I watch him every time I get a chance. Please help me welcome, once again, your youth speaker, Mrs. Denise Whalen.

She Told *Her* Story

Denise gathered items from her torn book bag and proceeded toward the podium. As she preceded down the aisle toward the front of the church, her twin children lifted their small thumbs up, as an expression of "go get 'em, Mom," and she received a gentle smile from her husband of many years, Malcolm Whalen. The church was still standing as she arrived at the podium and placed the items from her book bag on the glass surface.

"Thank you. Thank you." The applause continued. Denise had grown to be such a renowned speaker—a much sought-after leader by other churches and youth organizations. They loved the way she could captivate the youth as she told and retold her story. God had anointed her in such a marvelous way that, when she told the story, you would think that the events had just occurred. She was truly anointed. She sought the Lord much for such a fresh anointing before each appearance.

The audience was finally seated, and faces were all aglow with anticipation. People wondered what Denise would talk about this day. But of course, she had only one story—the *story*. "I am glad to be here today. I thank God for each of you pressing your way to be with me and my family today," she graciously commented.

"Where do I start," she pondered. "Today is Youth Day, and the title of my testimony is 'Full Circle,'" she stated. "I want to tell you my story. Many of you have heard my story but it never becomes stale. I have traveled throughout this region, telling the same story."

Immersed within the great crowd were a couple of teenagers whispering in the back, and even further to the back was another teenager already in the nodding position. Denise could only think of herself. She had been there and knew which road they were on. She knew their *final destination*—their final outcome if they did not turn back—because she had been there—lived it and relived it over and over again.

"Where do I start?" she questioned again. "As you all know, some years ago, I was kidnapped and placed in a truck. I could have been killed. Wait, wait. Let's go back further. It was Thanksgiving Day. I can still remember it so clear, just like it happened yesterday. I had planned it for months. I was to turn eighteen and wanted *out* of my parents' home. I was discontented and full of lust. I was completely possessed by the world. I wanted everything, and I do mean everything, that everyone else had. I wanted to be with the in-crowd. I snuck out at night. I drank, did drugs, and ran with those who did drugs. You name it, and I did it," Denise proclaimed. "I was wrong. All of it was wrong. It all grows old, and some don't live to tell about it. I had no idea what I was in for. Television is not real. Real life is what you have today, here, in this church. This is real. Making the Rapture is real. Being ready when Jesus comes, that is real. Everything else is false, false, false," she strongly proclaimed.

Rapture Crown

Don't let anybody steal your Rapture crown! Stand for God, now, as young people," emphasized Denise. "If I can persuade any one of you, stay home as long as you can. Live off your parents. Get an education. Learn. Be ready—make preparations for when you get out on your own. Life is hard, and you must be ready. Again, I say, you must be ready. Men will use you up, ladies, then what? What will you have to offer the man of your dreams if you are all used up—all spoiled and rotten?" questioned Denise.

Live or Die

"One night, I was in the back of a truck. I didn't know if I would live or die. As you may or may not have known, Malcolm, my husband, was once a drug dealer, and he made the decision to get out. How many of you know, once you get in, they don't let you out?" asked Denise.

She attempted to tell the captivated audience that dealing drugs most always leads to death. She spoke of when Malcolm had been shot and was legally dead for twenty minutes. "God, in His mercy, spared Malcolm's life and brought him back to life after twenty minutes," she said. "*He was dead.*"

The crowd's response was that of cheer and amazement. One would have thought that Denise never told this story, but she sought the Lord for a great anointing each time she revisited that time in her life. If it would save anyone, she wanted to relive it and relive it and relive it. God really blessed her to tell that story. She would make it so real.

God Had a Way

The sleeper from the back row sat up and started to pay close attention. The two teenagers from the back moved up closer. They didn't want to miss one word. The place was packed by this time. It was standing room only. God had a way of using Denise to draw the big crowds. It was amazing.

And when he came to himself, he said, How many hired servants of my father's have bread enough and to spare, and I perish with hunger! I will arise and go to my father, and will say unto him, Father, I have sinned against heaven, and before thee, And am no more worthy to be called thy son: make me as one of thy hired servants. And he arose, and came to his father. But when he was yet a great way off, his father saw him, and had compassion, and ran, and fell on his neck, and kissed him (Luke 15:17-20).

Now It All Made Sense

The two men remembered their last conversation with Malcolm and how they both had questioned an unlocked door on the building where they were holding Denise. The trunk, now they remembered, had been partially opened, *and now it all made sense*. She was gone! How far did she get? Did anyone pick her up? She had seen their faces. They had assumed that the drugs kept her unconscious, but they never doubled back to see if she was actually lying on the floor. She had made a run for it. She had escaped. God was helping her. He spared her life ... *again*.

Missing Person Report

"William!" shouted Sheila. William was in a daze, remembering that horrible day that Denise left home. "William!" shouted Denise again. Finally it appeared that her voice jolted him back into reality.

"Yes, Sheila. Now you have my attention, what do you want me to do?" answered William.

"We need to go down to the police station and put out a missing person report," stated Sheila.

"Ok, let's go," agreed William. They drove to the police station and gave all of the information known.

Prior to venturing out to the station, they summoned some of Denise's friends. Then they all gathered back at the Whalen home. Denise's friends were all afraid. They each took turns talking to Sheila and William. DeShaun and Sharon were both questioned. Star didn't seem to know a whole lot about

Denise's plans. "Mrs. Whalen, I told Denise not to do it. She really glamorized television and wanted what others had. I told her that life wasn't like TV. I am so sorry," stated DeShaun.

Crying almost until she lost her breath, Sharon was consumed with guilt. She had a major role in all of this. Sharon had encouraged Denise in her escapades and told Denise that she deserved better. "I told Denise that she deserved her freedom," sobbed Sharon. "I was so stupid. Please forgive me. I doubt that I could have changed her mind, but I know that she did listen to me. I knew the influence I had over Denise. I knew she sought my advice about stuff. She went out of her way to get Malcolm to notice her. Please, please, please find it in your hearts to forgive me. It is all clear to me now. I didn't know what I was saying to Denise then. It all just seemed like a joke. I didn't … mean for this to happen. Oh God. I won't forgive myself if something terrible happens to her."

"Sharon, listen to me. Denise is a big girl, and while you had influence over her, she had the final decision to do what she did in her life. I only pray that you will let this serve as a valuable lesson for you when dealing with others. Don't take part in their wrongdoings. Encourage people to do what is right. You know what is right," commented William. "Now, let's get down to the business of finding my daughter."

He Never Dreamed

"I have to do something. If it wasn't for me, Denise wouldn't be in this mess. If they harm her, I will never be able to live with myself. *It will be just another failure in my life*," thought Malcolm. "It's one thing to do foolish things, but when you involve others, you are also responsible for their outcome as well." Never in his wildest dreams did Malcolm fathom such an outcome. He never dreamed that it would come to this—Denise kidnapped and who knows what else? You know, that's the way the devil does you. He strings you along until he's done with you. He never endures the shame or punishment with you, but he leaves you to face it all alone.

William and Sheila went to file the incident report and returned home. Several hours later, the telephone rung at the Whalen's home. "Yes," answered William.

"Mr. Whalen, this is Officer Daniels. I understand that you filed a missing persons report?"

"Yes, I did," answered William.

"Mr. Whalen, something just came across my desk, and I will have to call you right back," stated the officer. He hung up the phone, and William just sat there, waiting for the next call.

The Door Wasn't Locked

The two men came to the conclusion that Denise had sneaked out of the abandoned building, and that was why the door wasn't locked. They thought she had concealed herself in the trunk, and that was why it was not locked. They relived the incident over and over again. They figured she had simply left the building and gotten a ride with them. Where was she? If found, she could lead the police to the vacant building and they would be arrested for kidnapping and many other charges.

"You idiot," screamed one man to the other.

"Hey, there you go again with all that screaming. Man, you always yelling at me. I am leaving this dump. I should have never listened to you."

"You are dumber than dumb! It's a little too late for that! Let's go and see if we can find her. We have to go back to that store where we bought the stuff, where the boys pulled us over."

"Oh, man I ain't going. Do you remember what the cops said they would do to us if they saw us out here again?"

"Oh, come on. It's too late to worry about the police. We are in trouble—no matter how you look at it. I should pop you. I should just blow your brains out right here and now!" shouted the other man.

"Yeah, right."

The God of Second Chances

"Oh, God, you are so good. You allowed me to get out of that building and into the back of that van unnoticed. I thank you, Lord," cried Denise. "I feel so foolish, Lord. I don't even have my Bible."

A voice shouted from the distance, "Hey, hey you. Do you need help?" Denise walked unaware of her surroundings. she was still in a daze. The voice shouted again, "Hey you are you injured?" The person realized that Denise was totally unaware of what was going on. The driver then pulled along the side of the road where Denise had been walking for some three hours now. It was only by God's grace no one else had stopped and tried to harm her. Lady." The driver walked a short distance behind Denise and grabbed her.

"Denise went into a rage. All of the fear, frustration, disappointment, and anger came gushing forth.

"Hey I am not trying to hurt you. What is your name? Look. I will show you my identification. My truck is right back there. Let me call you some help. My name is Andy. I was on my way home from church. I go there some evenings and clean up. Child, can you talk?" questioned Andy.

Denise was still screaming.

"What is your name?" shouted Andy.

"Don't hurt me, please. I need my mother. Call her. Please call her," cried Denise.

"Ok, we will do all of that. Come with me. Do you see my truck? It's right behind us. Here, let me wrap you in my jacket." They both walked back to his truck. It was more like Andy was carrying Denise. She was out of it. He loaded Denise into the truck, but Denise couldn't remember her name or her telephone number. She couldn't remember anybody's telephone number. Andy assumed she was in shock.

"You said you came from church?" asked Denise. "I use to be in church. As a matter of fact, I grew up in church. I had a good church. I miss my *book bag*."

"Your book bag?" questioned Andy.

"Yes," answered Denise. "My bible and all of my Christian literature was in there. You would think that I was studying at some theological school, but I kept those books in that book bag because I was ashamed for people to know that I was a Christian. I didn't want my friends to treat me funny, and after awhile, I just stopped trying." As Andy tried to get information from Denise, a van almost sideswiped him. He looked out the window, and it was the two guys. They didn't see Denise. They were speeding, but Denise was safe.

A Suspicious Van

"Mr. Whalen," asked the officer on the other end of the phone.

"Yes," replied William.

"I apologize that I had to hang up so abruptly, but I just got a call that a suspicious van was sighted on the west side of the city. I've sent someone to investigate. I will keep you posted," stated the officer.

"Thank you," replied William. As William hung up the phone, he slumped back in his chair and started crying.

Kill Malcolm

"There's one thing I am going to take care of before this all blows up in our faces," the man said.

"What's that?" questioned the other man.

"I am going to *kill Malcolm*—that's what I'm gon' do. Come on. Let's get over there. Denise is gone. I know she was weak. Maybe somebody hit her or even killed her."

"Yeah, let's get Malcolm."

What an Opportunity

Denise lifted her eyes from her prepared page to see the crowds' eyes all fixed her way. "I am grateful to be alive," she stated. "So many times during this ordeal, my life could have ended. I will never forget that horrible night when Malcolm was shot. I was waiting at the police station for my parents to come and get me when it came across the radio. Malcolm had been shot at his home, and *he was dead*. I don't remember much after that. I've been told the rest by my parents. You know it's funny—all that I wanted to get away from was what I needed all the time. Family, friends, and most importantly, God. These are the things that matter in this life. Neither money, drugs, nor fame could help me in my predicament, but God could, and God did." The crowd was on its feet applauding her. No one was left sitting down. With tear-stained eyes and a shaky voice, Denise continued, "Malcolm, did get this second chance in life, but at what price? My parents and Malcolm's parents went to the hospital and watched them work on him for what seemed to be several minutes. When it seemed that surely nothing else could be done, they removed all of the needles, tubes, and other apparatus, and Malcolm was still, when all of a sudden he started breathing again. Even though I was in the hospital and not there, I can only imagine. The men who took me will be in jail for a long, long time."

Grab the Kids

"Malcolm, come on. Mom and Dad will be waiting," stated Denise.

"Just one minute, let me grab the kids. You know we can't leave them behind," replied Malcolm.

Malcolm and Denise were all packed up and ready for a nice Sunday dinner at Sheila and William's house. They always went there, each Sunday, after Sunday service for some *down-home cookin'*. Denise and Malcolm hadn't missed a meal since they were married, several years earlier. This time, it wasn't a dream. It was real. Denise's life had truly come *full circle*!

Have You Failed God?

Rise up today, child of God. Have you done wrong? Have you failed God? Are you living in the past — past failures, past mistakes? Are you still failing God? Why not rise up like Peter did? He once walked the waters, only to fall. Now he was launching out into the deep. There is no need, if you have truly repented — repented with godly sorrow — to let the devil grind you with past failures, past mistakes. Look to God. Look to the hills from whence cometh your help. Think on the things of God. Seek His face more and more. Study His word. Let Jesus make Himself so real to you. Then you too will *"Stand up and lift up your voice"* to a lost and dying world, crying, *"Come and dine. Come dine. Come every one that thirsteth, come ye to the waters, and he that hath no money; come ye, buy and eat; yea, come, buy wine and milk without money and without price."*

Leave the past behind. Trust in the Lord with all of your heart. Let Him handle the rest of your tomorrows. **Trust in the LORD with all thine heart; and lean not unto thine own understanding. In all thy ways acknowledge him, and he shall direct thy paths** (Proverbs 3:5-6). Do not be deceived in any way. Follow hard after the Lord in this last and final hour. If you have neglected the love of God past failures and if you have lost that love along the way, seek the Lord with your whole heart and He will restore the joy, the joy of your salvation.

__Please repeat this simple prayer with me, asking Jesus to cleanse you of all unrighteousness__. He is able to restore, create, deliver, and most importantly, save you. He is willing. He is ready. He wants you, dear one. No one has ever loved you like Jesus. He does love you. Say:

Oh, God! I have sinned against you. I am so sorry! I have been away from home Lord and I'm ready to serve you, Lord, the rest of my life. I do believe. I do believe that you are able to deliver me and cleanse me from all hurt and pain of the past. I believe that the blood of your Son, Jesus Christ, can make me clean and whole, healing me. Come on into my heart and help me. Help me, Lord. I trust and believe that through the blood, I can make it. I do believe that I can make it with your help. Oh, Lord, __I want your help__. Save my soul. Love me, Jesus. I must have your love. Love me, Jesus. Jesus give me a new mind. Give me a mind that can reason with your word. Come on into my heart, Jesus! Come in!